STORM SHELTER

by Jon Mikkelsen
illustrated by Nathan Lueth

Librarian Reviewer
Marci Peschke
Librarian, Dallas Independent School District
MA Education Reading Specialist, Stephen F. Austin State University
Learning Resources Endorsement, Texas Women's University

Reading Consultant
Elizabeth Stedem
Educator/Consultant, Colorado Springs, CO
MA in Elementary Education, University of Denver, CO

STONE ARCH BOOKS
www.stonearchbooks.com

Keystone Books are published by Stone Arch Books
151 Good Counsel Drive, P.O. Box 669
Mankato, Minnesota 56002
www.stonearchbooks.com

Library of Congress Cataloging-in-Publication Data
Mikkelsen, Jon.
    Storm Shelter / by Jon Mikkelsen; illustrated by Nathan Lueth.
    p. cm. — (Keystone Books. We Are Heroes)
    ISBN 978-1-4342-0787-6 (library binding)
    ISBN 978-1-4342-0883-5 (pbk.)
    [1. Tornadoes—Fiction. 2. Dogs—Fiction. 3. Friendship—Fiction.
4. Lost and found possessions—Fiction.] I. Lueth, Nathan, ill. II. Title.
PZ7.M59268St 2009
[Fic]—dc22   2008008122

Summary: After a tornado ravages their neighborhood, three friends find
a stray dog and try to care for him. But someone seems to be hunting for
the dog.

Art Directior Heather Kindseth
Graphic Designer: Brann Garvey

J
MiK   OCLC   8/20/09

1 2 3 4 5 6 13 12 11 10 09 08

TABLE OF CONTENTS

Chapter 1

Usually, when Ben opened the door from the basement stairs, he saw the refrigerator, the oven, and his mom's flowers sitting in the kitchen window.

Today was different. When Ben opened the door from the basement, he saw a fallen tree. He saw puddles. He saw the sky.

The kitchen was gone.

Ben and his parents had been in the basement for safety while a big storm went through their neighborhood.

A tornado had roared through town. Most of the houses on Ben's block had been wrecked. Some had their roofs torn off. Others were missing walls and windows.

A huge oak tree had crashed through the living room window of the house next door to Ben's. At another house, two big trees had smashed through the roof.

Luckily no one was hurt. Neighbors walked through the streets picking up their belongings and comforting one another. It was still raining, but the storm was over.

Ben walked away from his house and looked down the street. His garage was still standing. That was good.

Just then, his best friend, Alison, was walking up the street toward him.

Alison ran over to Ben. "You're all right!" she said happily. She hugged him.

Ben nodded. "But our house isn't all right. Most of it is missing!" he said.

"That's awful," Alison said. "Ours has a lot of damage too. Have you seen Nathan?

Nathan was their other best friend. He also lived in the same neighborhood. "No," said Ben. "I was hoping you had seen him."

"There he is!" Alison shouted. She pointed behind Ben. Ben turned around and saw Nathan walking down the street with an umbrella.

"Hey, guys," Nathan said as he walked up. "My house is almost all gone."

"Half of our neighborhood is gone," said Ben.

Alison looked up into a tree across the street. The tornado had stripped most of the leaves from it, but there was something there. "What's that?" she asked.

The three friends walked across the street and looked up into the tree. There, perched on a branch, was a small brown and white dog. It barked and started to whimper.

Chapter 2

A SAFE SPOT

"It's a little dog," said Nathan.

"He's really cute," said Alison. "I think he might be hurt."

The dog barked again. It looked down at the ground and whimpered again. Nathan frowned. "I think there's something wrong with his leg," he said. "The dog looks like he's trying to jump but can't."

"What's a dog doing in a tree, anyway?" asked Ben. "Do you think he climbed up during the storm?"

"Dogs don't climb trees," Alison said. "I bet the tornado picked him up and dropped him in the tree. This dog is lucky to be alive."

"That's for sure," Nathan said.

"We have to help him," Alison told her friends.

A distant crack of thunder startled the dog. It lost its footing and stumbled. It tried to hold on to the branch, but its leg shook. The dog fell down to the soft, wet ground.

"Oh no!" said Alison. She ran over and looked down at the dog. "Are you okay, little dog?" she asked.

The dog tried to stand up. He shook as he stood. Then he lifted up his hurt paw.

"He doesn't look too badly hurt," said Nathan, "but I'm sure he's scared."

"He probably misses his owner," said Alison. She looked around. "I wonder who he belongs to," she said quietly.

"We should keep him safe until we can figure out who his owner is," Nathan said.

"That's a great idea," said Alison, "but we need a safe spot. Where are we going to keep him?"

"He doesn't look like he's going anywhere," said Ben.

He looked around. There was a plastic laundry basket on the ground nearby. "Let's carry him in this!" Ben suggested.

"Will the dog bite me if I pick him up?" Alison asked.

"Just be really careful," Nathan said. "Dogs usually only bite if they think they're being attacked."

Alison gently picked up the dog. She placed it in the laundry basket.

"I wonder where you belong," she said sadly.

"We should take him somewhere safe," Nathan said.

"We can go to my garage," said Ben. "It's safe. We can close the door, so the dog can't get out. Then we can try to find his home."

Suddenly, Alison thought of something. She gently lifted the dog's head and looked at his neck. The dog was wearing a collar, but it didn't have a tag on it.

"It doesn't say who he belongs to," she said sadly. "Maybe he's a stray dog."

"So he might not even have a home," Nathan said.

"Right," Alison said. "We have to take care of him until we find out where he belongs."

Chapter 3

The three friends ran to Ben's garage. Ben opened the door and they all went inside. He closed the door behind him.

"Now what do we do?" Nathan asked.

"We should try to help this poor dog's leg," Alison told him. "Ben," she asked, "do you have a first aid kit in this garage?"

Ben thought. "I think there's one in my dad's car," he told them. "I'll go find my dad and ask for the keys. Be right back."

Ben left the garage. Alison and Nathan stared at the dog. "I wonder what his name is," Alison said.

"We should give him a name," Nathan told her.

They looked at the dog. He had one white paw. His other paws were brown.

"Let's call him Lefty," Alison said. "His left paw in the front is white."

"That's a good name," Nathan said. He looked at the dog. "What do you think, Lefty?" Nathan asked.

The dog rolled onto its back. Then he stuck out his tongue.

Nathan smiled. "That means he wants his belly rubbed," he told Alison. "So I guess that means he likes his new name."

Just then, Ben came back. He was out of breath from running. He slammed the door behind him and locked it. "You guys, I think the dog is in trouble," he said nervously.

"What do you mean?" Alison asked.

"When I was getting the keys, I saw someone talking to my dad," Ben said. "A man. He was looking for a small white and brown dog."

"That's great!" Alison said. "It must be Lefty's owner!"

"Who's Lefty?" Ben asked.

"We named the dog while you were gone," Nathan explained.

"Well, I don't think this person was Lefty's owner," Ben told them. "My dad asked what the dog's name was, and the man said he wasn't sure."

"Do you think someone is trying to dognap Lefty?" Alison asked quietly. She looked worried.

"I don't know," Ben said. "But I think we better keep Lefty in here, just to be on the safe side."

There was a small glass window in the door. Alison looked out of the window. A strange man was down the street, talking to one of Ben's neighbors. He didn't look happy.

In the laundry basket, Lefty barked.

"Be quiet, Lefty!" Alison said quickly. "You might be in danger. We can't let anyone know you're here!"

Chapter 4

HIDE HIM!

"Did you get the keys so we can get the first aid kit?" Nathan asked Ben. "We should try to wrap up his leg."

Ben opened the car door and handed a small white box to Nathan. "Here's the first aid kit," he said.

"Alison, you hold Lefty while I wrap his hurt leg," Nathan said. "Ben, you keep watch by the window."

Ben walked to the window and looked out. Alison picked up Lefty and held him, gently, in her arms. "Do you think he'll bite?" she asked.

Nathan shrugged. "He might," he said. "After all, he's hurt. Hold his mouth closed with one of your hands. Just pet him gently and I'll be really careful."

Alison carefully held the dog's mouth closed. Lefty looked scared, but he stayed still. Nathan opened the first aid box and took out a roll of white bandages. He slowly and carefully wrapped the bandage around Lefty's hurt leg. When the leg was wrapped up, he taped the bandage closed.

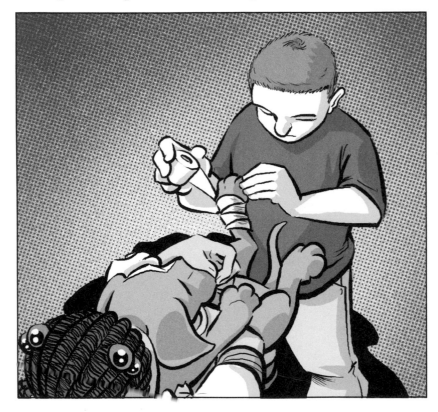

"Okay, you can put him back in the laundry basket," Nathan said.

Alison placed Lefty back into the laundry basket. "That was great, Nathan!" she said. "How did you know how to do that?"

"We had a dog when I was little," Nathan said. "Once, she hurt her leg and this is what my dad did to help her."

Just then, Ben whispered, "Hide him! Hide Lefty! The man is coming toward the garage!"

Chapter 5

Alison picked up the laundry basket with Lefty in it. Then she climbed into Ben's dad's car and shut the door.

A moment later, Ben's dad and the strange man were at the garage door. Ben's dad knocked on the window.

Nathan and Ben looked at each other. "We better let them in," Ben said. "Otherwise, they will know we have Lefty."

Nathan nodded. Ben opened the door.

"What are you kids doing?" Ben's dad asked.

"Just talking about the storm," Nathan said quickly.

"We wanted to stay inside, just in case," Ben added.

"Have either of you seen a small dog around?" Ben's dad asked.

"What does the dog look like?" Nathan asked.

The strange man frowned at Nathan. "Have you seen more than one dog?" he asked.

"Um . . . no," Nathan said. "I was just wondering."

"Boys, this is Mr. Weber, from the humane society," Ben's dad said. "One of their dogs was outside in the yard when the storm started, and he was picked up by the tornado. They're hoping he landed somewhere in this neighborhood and is okay."

Ben and Nathan looked at each other. "You're from the humane society?" Nathan asked. "The one that keeps stray animals and finds homes for them?"

"That's right," the man said quietly. "This dog was our favorite. We hadn't found a home for him yet, but he'll be a great pet for the right family. I really hope I can find him. We called him Lefty, because his front left paw was white, but the others were brown."

Just then, a bark came from the parked car. Nathan and Ben heard Alison whisper, "Be quiet, Lefty!"

Mr. Weber looked at the car. "Is someone in there?" he asked loudly.

Ben's dad walked over and opened the car door. Slowly, Alison got out. "Please don't hurt him," she said. "I really like Lefty."

Ben smiled. "Mr. Weber, we do have your dog," he said. "And I think Alison might know of a great family for him."

Nathan explained, "Alison, this man works for the humane society."

Alison smiled widely. "Can I keep Lefty?" she asked quietly.

"If your parents come to the shelter and agree, then you can," Mr. Weber said.

Nathan said, "We can't have a dog anymore, because my mom is allergic. But I really like dogs. Maybe I could come and help sometimes."

Alison pointed to Lefty's hurt leg. "Nathan did a great job of helping Lefty," she told Mr. Weber.

"I'd like to help too," Ben said.

Mr. Weber smiled. "This was a bad day because of the storm," he said. "But now it's a great day for dogs. Lefty might have a new home, and we have new volunteers for the animal shelter!"

ABOUT THE AUTHOR

Jon Mikkelsen has written dozens of plays for kids, which have involved aliens, superheroes, and more aliens. He acts on stage and loves performing in front of an audience. Jon also loves sushi, cheeseburgers, and pizza. He loves to travel, and has visited Moscow, Berlin, London, and Amsterdam. He lives in Minneapolis and has a cat named Coco, who does not pay rent.

ABOUT THE ILLUSTRATOR

Nathan Lueth has been a freelance illustrator since 2004. He graduated from the Minneapolis College of Art and Design in 2004, and has done work for companies like Target, General Mills, and Wreked Records. Nathan was a 2008 finalist in Tokyopop's Rising Stars of Manga contest. He lives in Minneapolis, Minnesota.

GLOSSARY

allergic (uh-LUR-jik)—if you are allergic to something, it causes you to sneeze, develop a rash, or have another unpleasant reaction

attacked (uh-TAKD)—tried to hurt

bandage (BAN-dij)—a piece of cloth or material that is wrapped around an injured part of the body to protect it

collar (KOL-ur)—a thin band of material worn around the neck of a dog or cat

dognap (DOG-nap)—to steal a dog

humane society (hyoo-MANE suh-SYE-uh-tee)—a group that protects animals

neighborhood (NAY-bur-hud)—a group of homes

strange (STRAYNJ)—unfamiliar, not known

stray (STRAY)—a lost cat or dog

tornado (tor-NAY-doh)—a violent, whirling column of air that appears as a dark cloud

volunteers (vol-uhn-TEERZ)—people who do a job for free

whimper (WIM-pur)—to make weak, crying noises

DISCUSSION QUESTIONS

1. Why did Nathan, Ben, and Alison think that Mr. Weber wanted to dognap Lefty?

2. Do you think the three friends did the right thing when they brought Lefty to the garage? What would you have done?

3. In this book, the three kids decide to become volunteers at the animal shelter. Where would you like to volunteer? Why?

WRITING PROMPTS

1. Have you ever been through a big storm? What was it like? What happened?

2. Do you have any pets? Write about your pet. If you don't have one, write about a pet you might like to have.

3. The three kids in this book are best friends. Write about your best friend. What do you like about him or her? What do you do together?

MORE ABOUT ADOPTING AN ANIMAL

Animal shelters all over the United States are full of animals that don't have homes. Many of these animals are ready for adoption. If a family wants a dog or cat, the family can go to the shelter and pick out a pet.

But animal shelters themselves need help. It takes a lot of time, money, and energy to make sure an animal shelter is providing the right care for helpless animals. If you ever thought of caring for animals, a shelter is a great place to start.

First, check your local phone book. Look under Animal Shelter, Humane Society, or Animal Control. Call up a few places and see if they need volunteers.

Some volunteers help walk the animals.
Dogs and cats need exercise and fresh air.
Volunteers take the animals out of their cages,
and sometimes go for walks. It gives the
animals breaks in their lonely days.

The best thing about being a volunteer at
an animal shelter is getting to know the
animals themselves. You'll learn a lot about
different breeds of dogs and cats, watch how
they express their different personalities, and
understand more about the care required to
take care of a pet.

You can make a difference in an animal's life!

INTERNET SITES

Do you want to know more about subjects related to this book? Or are you interested in learning about other topics? Then check out FactHound, a fun, easy way to find Internet sites.

Our investigative staff has already sniffed out great sites for you!

Here's how to use FactHound:

1. Visit *www.facthound.com*

2. Select your grade level.

3. To learn more about subjects related to this book, type in the book's ISBN number: **9781434207876**.

4. Click the **Fetch It** button.

FactHound will fetch the best Internet sites for you!